CLOUD BUSTING

www.**kidsatrandomhouse**.co.uk/malorieblackman

www.malorieblackman.co.uk

CLOUD BUSTING

MALORIE BLACKMAN

CORGI YEARLING BOOKS

CLOUD BUSTING
A CORGI YEARLING BOOK 0 44 086677 4

First published in Great Britain by Doubleday, 2004
an imprint of Random House Children's Books

This edition published for Scholastic 2005

1 3 5 7 9 10 8 6 4 2

Set in 14/20pt Garamond by
Falcon Oast Graphic Art Ltd.

RANDOM HOUSE CHILDREN'S BOOKS
61–63 Uxbridge Road, London W5 5SA
A division of The Random House Group Ltd

RANDOM HOUSE AUSTRALIA (PTY) LTD
20 Alfred Street, Milsons Point, Sydney,
New South Wales 2061, Australia

RANDOM HOUSE NEW ZEALAND LTD
18 Poland Road, Glenfield, Auckland 10, New Zealand

RANDOM HOUSE (PTY) LTD
Endulini, 5A Jubilee Road, Parktown 2193, South Africa

THE RANDOM HOUSE GROUP Limited Reg. No. 954009
www.kidsatrandomhouse.co.uk

A CIP catalogue record for this book is available from the British Library.

Printed and bound in Great Britain by
Cox & Wyman Ltd, Reading, Berkshire.

To Neil and Lizzy, with my love.
And thanks, Lizzy, for the phrase 'Fizzy Feet',
which was the inspiration for this book.
I love you.
'Dare to be different.'

Contents

MR MACKIE SAID

Mr Mackie said,
'Write a poem
About
Someone near to you,
Dear to you.
A pet,
A family member,
A friend.'
Funny, I thought,
How pets come first.
'That's your homework,'
Said Mr Mackie.
And the whole class groaned.
Except me.
'But poems are hard, sir!'
'Poems are boring!'
'Poems are for old people.'
'Poems are for boring, old people.'

'No one reads poetry –
Unless their teacher makes them.'
'No one likes poetry except
Poets –
Or those who don't have a life.'
And Mr Mackie said,
'ENOUGH!'
And we all went quiet
'Cause Mr Mackie sure can shout.
Then Mr Mackie said,
'Hands up those who like rap music.'
And me and some others
Put our hands up.
'Hands up those who like pop music.'
And me and most others
Put our hands up.
'Hands up those who like classical
    music.'

And me and almost everyone
Kept our hands down.
Except for Oliver.
Only Oliver
Put his hand up.
But then he would.
And Mr Mackie said,
'Rap music and pop
And punk and rock
Have words.
And the words are poetry
Set to music,
That's all.'
'What about classical music?'
Asked Oliver.
But then he would.
'Classical music creates poetry
In your mind.

And your heart.
And your soul.
Even if there are no words
Being sung or spoken,
It still creates poetry
Inside you.'
And we all went quiet
Thinking.
Thinking.
And the strange thing is
No one laughed.
Mr Mackie smiled.
'Any questions?'
Hands shot up.
'Does it have to rhyme, sir?'
'No.'
'How do we start, sir?'
'With whatever comes

Into your head.
Just let it out.
Don't hold back.
Don't stop yourselves.
Don't censor yourselves.
Let your words flow
Like a mountain stream
Like a babbling brook
Like a raging river
Like a tidal wave
A tsunami!
Like a cosmic wave,
Moving between galaxies.
Like a . . . like a . . .'
And we all groaned
'Cause Mr Mackie was off
Like a racehorse
Running its own race.

Just running 'cause it can,
Running to hear its hooves
Pound the ground.
Just running, running
For love and pleasure.
'Sir, can I write about
My dog?
My cat?
My goldfish?'
'Yes.'
'Sir, can I write about
My computer?
My skateboard?
Jaws, my teddy bear?'
'No.'
I put my hand up.
'Sir, can I write about Davey?'
The class went very still . . .

Very quiet.
My face began to burn
Burn hot then
Burn cold.
'Yes, Sam, you do that,'
Said Mr Mackie after the longest
    pause.
'Write about Dave.'
'What d'you want to write
About him for?'
That was Alex,
Talking at me.
Frowning at me.
Davey made him nervous,
Uncomfortable.
Uneasy.
Because of what he did.
Even though Davey isn't

Here any more
He still has the power
To make people
Uncomfortable,
Uneasy,
. . . to remember.
I didn't answer
My ex-best friend Alex.
What could I say?
I want to write about Davey
Because Mum says
You don't miss the water
Till the well runs dry.
I want to write about Davey
Because when he was here
I never gave him a second thought.
I want to write about Davey
Because now he's gone

I can't get him out of my head.
And I never thought I would,
But I miss him.
There!
I admit it.
He's gone.
And it's *his* fault –
The fault of the class idiot
The class bully.
And I miss him.
Not the class idiot.
He's gone too and
I don't miss him one bit.
I miss Davey.
His name was Davey.
Dave.
David Youngson.
But everyone called him Fizzy Feet.

WHAT'S IN A NAME?

What's in a name? Not much.
That's what the class idiot said
After Davey's name
Was changed to Fizzy Feet.

It happened in assembly –
The second or third morning
After the long summer break,
About seven or eight months ago.

Maybe less, maybe more.
It was a long time ago,
But memories are longer.
Davey sat in front of me.

His light-brown hair
Wasn't long enough
To hide the frayed collar
Of his shirt.

His navy-blue school jumper
Had a small hole
At the elbow.
I shook my head and turned away.

My mum would never
Let me leave home
With holes at my
Elbows. No way!

Davey was the new boy,
Full of uncertain smiles
And anxious eyes
And not much else.

My best friend Alex
Sat next to me
On my right
Playing with his Gameboy.

16

And on my left
Alicia. A-lic-i-a!
A name like April showers
Dropping gently onto spring flowers.

(Not that I'll leave in
The bit about Alicia
When I hand this poem
To Mr Mackie. No way!)

Mrs Spencer, the head,
Was droning on
And on
And on . . .

I was sleeping
With my eyes open
When it happened.
Waking us all up.

Davey jumped up,
Fell sideways
And started rubbing his legs
Saying, 'Fizzy feet! I've got fizzy feet!'

We didn't have a clue
What he was talking about.
Mr Mackie ran over
To sort him out.

'Dave, what's the matter?
What's wrong?
What's going on?'
Mr Mackie was all concern.

'Fizzy feet!
I've got fizzy feet!'
Davey pulled off his shoes
And rubbed his toes. (What a pong!)

'What're you talking about?'
Mr Mackie began to frown.
'D'you mean you've got
Pins and needles?'

'Ow! Yes, that's what I said, sir!
Fizzy feet!'
A moment's stunned silence.
Then we all roared like we had toothache.

Mr Mackie ranted
Mr Mackie raved
Mr Mackie was not happy
As he escorted Davey from the hall.

Fizzy feet,
Dizzy, fizzy feet
Busy, dizzy, fizzy feet
What a dork!

Davey never lived that down.
The class bully
Wouldn't let him.
What a dork.

Davey hated the name
Fizzy Feet
But what could he do about it?
Not much. Nothing.

The class bully wouldn't let him.

FACING THE TRUTH – WITH HAIKUS

Mr Mackie said,
'Today, you lucky people,
We're doing haikus!'

'What's one of them, sir?'
'Poems to stir the senses,
Plus, they're very short.

A mere three lines long
Just seventeen syllables
Simple, pimple – right?

Three lines made up of
Words which are five syllables
Then seven, then five.'

'Haikus,' Alex groaned.
'What a waste of time and space.'
I didn't think so.

'Japanese poems.
Haikus . . .' sighed Mr Mackie.
'A pure, paced rhythm.'

'But sir,' said Alex,
'Haikus mean lots of counting.
That's not fair! That's maths!'

'Haikus are art, child.
Full of heart, soul and passion
So let your mind soar.'

'To where? And what for?'
'To the stars and beyond, child.'
'And when I land, sir?'

Mr Mackie frowned,
Scratched his head and frowned some more.
'You'll have memories.'

'Big deal!' Alex scoffed.
And that was the end of that.
Haikus bit the dust.

Haiku for Davey:

We should've been friends
But the bad thing that happened
To you changed my life.

DESCRIPTIONS

The class bully was
A mean, mad moron
An insane idiot
A dopey dweeb
A prize poop-head
A narrow-minded no-hoper
A hurtful, horrible person.
And everyone knew it.

The class beauty was
Alicia.
Gorgeous
A great singer
A great looker
Funny
Talented
Keen on Fizzy Feet – called him Dave.

Fizzy Feet was
Good and tall
Good and skinny
Good and quiet
A good laugh (according to Alicia)
Good at maths
Good at being friendly
Not so good with the class bully
   though.

POEMS POSTED AROUND THE SCHOOL – BY YOU KNOW WHO

When I see scabby Dave, how I laugh!
He's got legs like a knock-kneed giraffe
And his bum is so smelly
It appeared on the telly
'Cause he never once gets in the bath.

There once was a moron called Dave
Who belonged in a zoo or a cave
He had holes in his clothes
And snot in his nose
And his eyebrows could do with a shave.

Said directly to Fizzy Feet:
You're a big dork-head called Davey
You're thicker than twelve-day-old gravy
My dog did a poo
That was smarter than you
From your breath, I wish someone would
   save me!

'Pick it up,
Fizzy Feet.'
Fizzy Feet
Picked it up.
'Give it here,
Fizzy Feet.',
Fizzy Feet
Gave it up.
The bully despised Davey
For a coward and a meekling.
He gave Dave so much grief and hurt.
He thought Dave was a weakling.
So whenever it would suit him
He would gladly put the boot in.

STANDING PROUD

Davey never shouted, never bolted,
He stood his ground, he watched and he
   waited,
He did not seem to realize the effect
Just standing there, not uttering a word
Had on the class bully, the school bully.
A faint, sad smile would play across his
   lips
As he stood before the one who hurt him.
A smile that just had to be wiped away,
Washed away, knocked away, smashed far
   away,
But Davey just stood proud and never
   spoke.

THE TRUTH HURTS

I want to tell you the truth
Time to tell you the truth
Cards on the table
Get it off my chest
Open my mind and
Reveal all!
The class bully
The class moron
The class idiot
His name was Sam
In case you haven't already guessed
I am Sam
Sam is me
I'm the one who made
Davey's life a misery.

SETTING THE SCENE

It was a strange day
Some sunshine
Some rain
Some cloud
Some blue sky
A mixed bag.
Roll up, roll up
Dip your hand in
And pull out
Any kind of weather.

Fizzy Feet lived two doors down
From the class bully – me.
Our mums became great friends.
They wanted their sons to be good friends
   too.
Every morning Mum said,
'Sam, why don't you go and knock for Dave?'
'I don't want to walk to school with him,'
I sniffed. 'Davey's a dork!'

'Go and be friendly,' Mum insisted.
So I'd knock for Davey, with my mum
   watching.
And once we'd turned the corner
I'd make Davey pay.
But one rainy morning . . . I went too far.
I was just mucking about
I didn't mean to hurt him
Not seriously hurt him

But I pushed him
And Davey snapped
And pushed me back
And I tripped
And I slipped
And I fell backwards
Into the path of an oncoming car
And the car didn't have time to stop . . .

I heard brakes screech
And someone scream
And then . . . a hand came out of
    nowhere
And grabbed me
And pulled me out of harm's way.
Seconds came and went before I
Realized what had happened.
Davey had saved my life.

Davey had actually saved my life.
The driver tooted her horn
And shook an angry fist
But she didn't stop.
She didn't even slow down.
A man, a pedestrian asked me,
'Are you OK?'
I didn't answer. Couldn't answer.

I couldn't hear a thing
Over the thundering of my heart.
And then Davey smiled
Just smiled. And turned to the man,
   the pedestrian
And said, 'My friend is fine.'
And I felt so strange
'Cause we weren't friends
And Davey had saved my life.

And all I could think was,
'Why did he do it?'
And all I could feel was
I'M ALIVE. Thank God!
And all I could hear was
My heart stomping in my chest
And all I could see was
Davey's smile.

And in that moment, I hated that smile
Almost as much as I hated Davey
Because he'd saved my life
And then he made it worse.
He said, 'Your life belongs to me now.'
And he had a strange look on his face.
'What d'you mean?' I hissed at him.
And Davey smiled his smile.

'I have to take care of you
Make sure no harm comes to you.
I have to look after you
Your life belongs to me.
I have to show you things
I have to teach you things
I have to be with you
Your life belongs to me.'

'Get real!' I scoffed.
'My life belongs to you?
Yeah, right!' But inside,
Inside I was scared.
Davey's smile did it.
How I wished he'd stop smiling.
For just five minutes, five seconds.
I stormed off.

Anything to get away from him
But Davey ran after me.
'Look at that,' he pointed.
'A blunt rainbow.'
'A what?' I looked up.
I couldn't help it.
And I saw something
I'd never noticed before.

The short, sharp burst of rain
Had turned to drizzle,
Drops shining like pearls
Through the sunlit air
And a muted rainbow
Danced in and out
Of the scattered, grey-white clouds.
A blunt rainbow.

And it was like
My eyes weren't my eyes
But Davey's.
And it was like
My mind wasn't my own
But Davey's.
And it was like
Nothing I'd ever felt before.

My head was full of words
That I'd never used before.
I could see things in the rain
And the clouds and the sky
That weren't there before.
Or maybe I'd just
Never noticed them before.
I didn't like it – at all.

So I ran
And ran
And ran
And ran
And ran
And ran
To school
Away from *him*.

SHADOW

After that, Davey became
My shadow.

He followed me around
Like my shadow.

In front of my friends
He was still Fizzy Feet.

But when it was just us two
He became Davey.

Davey who cracked such bad jokes
That I couldn't help laughing.

And he said, 'Your smile is so big,
It's going to fall off your face.'

Davey who said my mum's cooking
Tasted of sunshine and rainbows.

And made her grin
And strut like a peacock.

'What a sweet boy that Davey is!'
Said Mum. She admired his taste.

Davey who said Dad's home-made table
Was the best he'd ever seen

Even though Mum said a silent prayer
Whenever she put anything on it

Heavier than a chocolate biscuit.
As a table it was a dead loss.

'What a smart boy that Davey is!'
Said Dad. He admired Davey's sense.

And when we were alone
When it was just Davey and me

He'd ask, 'D'you know what stars are?
Stars are holes in the floor of heaven.'

He'd ask, 'D'you know what dreams are?
Dreams are a way for us to live two lives.'

'Huh?' I frowned, my mouth turned down.
What was he talking about? Did he even know?

'I read about a man,' said Davey,
'Who once dreamt that he was a butterfly.

Butterfly, flutter by
Gently with the breeze
As it blows you with its ease
Through the flowers, past the trees
So butterfly, flutter by
Flutter by, butterfly.'

'Did you make that up?' I asked,
Wondering how we'd got onto this subject.

'Yes, I did,' smiled Davey.
'It shows,' I replied sourly.

Davey grinned at me. 'So anyway,
This man once dreamt he was a butterfly

And he woke up and wondered
If he was a man who'd dreamt

He was a butterfly. Or a butterfly
Who was now dreaming he was a man.'

'Davey, where d'you get this stuff from?
You're making my head hurt,' I groaned.

'I read it, see it, think it, hear it, taste it . . .'
'Taste it?'

'What's your favourite food?' Davey asked.
'Roast lamb – the way my mum makes it –

And rice. And roast parsnips
The way my mum makes them.'

I licked my lips at the thought.
'And what does it taste like?' asked Davey.

I frowned. 'Roast lamb and rice tastes like . . .
Roast lamb and rice.'

'Use your imagination,' Davey urged.
'When you eat it, how does it make you feel?

What does it remind you of?
What thoughts enter your head as you eat?'

I considered. 'I think, what lovely
Roast lamb and rice!'

'Doesn't it taste like star beams on your tongue?
Or daydreams in your mouth?

Or wishes down your throat?
Or happiness in your stomach? Or . . .'

'Or a headache in my brain,' I grumbled.
Davey was really making my head hurt.

'There's more than one way
To look at something,' said Davey, adding,

'I know you think I'm different,
Unique, special, individual . . .'

'The word I'm thinking of is "weird"!' I said.
Davey grinned, 'Well, I'm glad.

The worse thing in the world –
No, the worse thing in the universe

Would be to look and walk and talk
And think like everyone else.'

I looked at Davey then
Really looked at him.

And I realized something strange.
He meant every word.

And even though talking to Davey
Sometimes did my head in,

At least he had something to say
A way that was all his own.

I guess what I'm trying to say is
He wasn't the least bit boring.

Alex and I talked about football,
And other sports.

Football results
And films sometimes.

Football players
And girls sometimes.

Football tactics
And school sometimes.

But mainly football
Mostly football.

Davey and I talked about
The Earth as a football

The stars as spectators.
Girls as aliens

Teachers as robots
Or nut-bags, or demons.

Films to walk into,
Books to hold onto

Music to live for,
Eminem and Mozart

Jobs to grow up for,
Dreams to stay young with.

Davey and I talked about
Anything and everything.

I tried to be careful
I really and truly did

But people started to notice
That we were sometimes together,

Often together,
Always together.

My best friend Alex said,
'You're spending a lot of time

With Fizzy Feet.
What's that about?'

'I can't stand him,' I panicked.
'So why would I hang around with him?

He's a first class, grade A,
Top-of-the-dung-heap moron.'

And Alex started laughing at something,
Someone behind me.

And I turned
And there was Davey

And he'd heard every word.
He didn't say anything

He just walked away.
And Alex was still laughing.

And I looked at Alex
And I looked at Davey walking away

And at that moment
I had to choose

To choose between the kind of boy I was
And the kind of boy I wanted to be.

I chose to stay with Alex.
I watched Davey walk away

And I knew I was making the wrong choice
But my feet wouldn't move.

I didn't want Alex and my mates
To laugh at me as well

So I stayed with Alex
And watched Davey walk away.

And then I realized
That Davey wasn't my shadow

It was the other way round.

SORRY

I walked home
All alone
Thinking, 'Dave, I'm sorry.

That wasn't nice.'
My mum's advice?
'Go and say you're sorry.'

I told her, 'No.
I will not go
And tell him that I'm sorry.'

'But it was mean.
You should be keen
To let him know you're sorry.'

I dug in my heels
Despite appeals
To admit that I was sorry.

'There's no TV,
No treats for tea
Until you say you're sorry.'

'I'm sorry now
You rotten cow!
Sorry! Sorry! Sorry!'

I had a shout.
Now there's no doubt
That I am very, very,
Very, very, very
Very sorry.

No Big Deal

The next day Davey
Passed my door
Without stopping.
I ran out and said
'Wait up, Davey.'
But he kept walking.
And there I was
Running after him
And he wouldn't stop.
So by the time I
Reached him
I was puffed
And annoyed
With both him
And me.
'Didn't you hear
Me calling you?'
I ranted between

Gasps to fill my lungs.
And he looked at me
Just looked at me
And I spent a lifetime
Which lasted no more
Than a second
Thinking about all
The things he could say
To me
In response
In reply,
All the things I deserved
To hear.
But he smiled,
Just smiled
And said, 'Hi.'
I felt strange – embarrassed.
I looked away,

But didn't walk away.
I caught sight of
Davey's break box
In his hand.
He'd started his break early.
Like just after breakfast.
'What've you got?' I asked,
Digging into my bag
For my own break box.
I opened mine up
So we could both look
And compare snacks.
He had carrot sticks,
A thick chunk of cucumber,
Bread sticks
Grapes
And an apple.
I had salt and vinegar crisps

Chocolate buttons
A packet of peanuts
And an apple.
'I'll swap you my peanuts
For your cucumber,'
I said.
I love cucumber.
It's the only green thing
I'll eat.
'I can't eat peanuts,'
said Davey. 'I'm allergic.'
I frowned.
I didn't really get it.
'I'm allergic to peanuts,'
said Davey. 'But I'll swap you
Your packet of
Chocolate buttons
For all my cucumber.'

'Fifteen buttons,'
I haggled.
'The packet has probably
Only got ten in it
In the first place,'
Davey pointed out.
So I gave him the packet
And took his cucumber.
And we carried on
Munching and crunching
As we walked.
'Don't tell anyone
About my allergy,'
Said Davey after a while.
'Why not?' I asked.
'I don't want a fuss,'
Shrugged Dave.
'Promise me

You won't tell.'
So I promised.
No problem.
No big deal.
But the promise
Left my mouth
Escaped my mind
Fizzled out
Sizzled out
And I forgot it.
Pure forgot it.
Clean forgot it.
Left it.
Lost it.
Just forgot it.

BIG MISTAKE

I told Alex
Big Mistake
About Davey's allergy
Big Mistake
'How allergic is he?'
Big Mistake
'I don't know,' I said.
Big Mistake
'He didn't run away screaming
Big Mistake
From my packet of peanuts
Big Mistake
If that's what you mean.'
Big Mistake
I was sorry I spoke.
Big Mistake
'I might've guessed,
Big Mistake

That he'd have more
Big Mistake
Than his fizzy feet wrong with him,'
Big Mistake
said Alex, scornfully.
Big Mistake
'My cousin Gennifer has an allergy,'
Big Mistake
Said Pete thoughtfully. 'She's very allergic
Big Mistake
To cat hairs. They make her sneeze and
    sneeze.'
Big Mistake.
'Sneeze, eh,' said Alex just as thoughtfully.
Big Mistake
And I thought, 'Oh no! I know that look.
Big Mistake
He's just had an idea. He's going to do
    something to Davey.'

92

Big Mistake
Telling him about Davey's allergy was a
BIG MISTAKE.

Too Hot

My world was too hot.
The country was too hot.
The city was too hot.
The street was too hot.
The school was too hot.
The classroom was too hot.
My clothes were too hot.
My skin was too hot.
My blood was too hot.
Watching Alex whisper and laugh
With Pete, was making my insides
Too hot.

JUST A JOKE

'Hi, Davey,' said Alex.
'Would you like one of my crisp sandwiches?'
Davey looked up from his break box,
Surprised.
He wasn't the only one.
I looked at Alex
Surprised and suspicious
Suspicious and surprised.
Alex wasn't usually nice to Davey.
What was he up to?

'What flavour crisps?' Davey asked
Through a smile big enough
To turn upside down and
Shelter under, out of the rain.
Alex was talking to him
Alex was offering to share a sandwich with him.
Davey was so happy.

My insides were about to melt.
'Cheese and onion,' said Alex. 'My mum
Makes them special. You'll love them.'
'Yes, please,' said Davey.
Davey reached out for the sandwich
Alex held out to him.
'Oh no,' said Alex. 'I'll hold it.
Your hands might not be clean.
You can eat half and
I'll have the other half.
That's fair, isn't it?'
I stood up, my heart dive-bouncing
Like a bungee jumper.

'Yes, that's fair,' said Davey.
And he took a bite. One bite.
And he chewed with a smile.
And swallowed with a frown.

And the whole class watched.
The very air held its breath.
As Davey started to cough.
And Alex cracked up laughing.
And Davey coughed harder.
And Alex laughed more.

But then the laughing stopped,
As Davey's hands flew to his throat
Tearing at his skin
Clawing at the invisible hands
Choking him from the inside out.
His face erupted in red blotches.
The whites of his eyes were turning red
He couldn't breathe.
He fell to his knees, his eyes on me,
And Alicia screamed.

Lucy ran to get help,
Claudia started to shriek.
Martin shouted at Alex.
'It was only one peanut,' cried Alex.
'I only put one peanut in there.
It was just a joke.
I thought he'd sneeze.
It was just a joke.'
Davey fell on his side, his eyes on me.
And was still.

I ran over to Davey
To loosen his shirt collar
But it was already undone
And Davey was so still.
Mr Mackie ran into the room
Holding a fat, grey pen.
He pushed us out of the way

And took the top off the pen
Before jamming the other end
Into Davey's thigh.

'Come on, Davey. Please,'
Begged Mr Mackie.
But Davey was so still.
Mr Mackie kept the pen
Against Davey's thigh
For long, long seconds.
'It was only a joke, sir,'
Said Alex. 'I only meant it as a joke.'
And he started to cry.
Great, big, rolling tears as he watched
   Davey.

'Lucy, run to the office
And tell them to phone
For an ambulance,'
said Mr Mackie. 'And
For God's sake – hurry.'
I turned to Alex
And saw myself
And hated what I saw.
I hated Alex so much.
But I hated myself more.

And Davey's eyes were on me.
Still watching me.
Still.

FINE

Davey was OK.
The pen Mr Mackie
Jabbed into his leg
Was a special pen
Full of adrenalin.
It did the trick.
By the time
The ambulance arrived
Davey was no longer
Unconscious.
He said he was OK.
'I'm fine, Mr Mackie.
I'm fine.'
But his face was still red,
And his lips were swollen
And he couldn't stand up
And he kept scratching his skin.

Mr Mackie
Insisted that he went
To the hospital.
Davey's mum was going
To meet him there.

As the school secretary
Helped Davey out
Of the classroom,
Mr Mackie closed the door
And turned to me
And said, 'Sam, tell me
Exactly what's been going on.
NOW.'
So I did. Every detail.

Mr Mackie picked up
Alex's sandwich
From the floor
Where it'd fallen
And opened it.
One more peanut
Sat in amongst
The crisps
On the other side
Of the sandwich.
Mr Mackie was so angry.
Alex was still crying.
Mr Mackie took Alex out
To see the Head.

Whilst he was gone
I turned around
And everyone was looking at me,

Eyes on me again.
'It wasn't my fault,'
I whispered helplessly,
Hopelessly.
'If I knew what Alex was up to
I'd have stopped him.'
A few eyes turned away at that
In disgust? In disbelief?
Why didn't anyone believe me?
Davey was my friend.
I wouldn't've let Alex do it.
But no one knew Davey was my friend
Because I didn't want anyone to know.

They thought I was with Alex.
Like Alex.
Another Alex.
No, they thought I was Sam.

Worse than Alex.
And they were all right.
I was worse because
I was a coward.
Davey could be my friend
As long as no one found out.
As long as no one knew.
Just him and me.
Just me and him.
Davey, just you and me.
Me and you.
A secret to be shared by two.

I ran from the room
I escaped to the toilets
I locked the door
And lowered the lid
And sat down

And looked down at my shoes
And watched the water
Fall from my eyes,
Escape from my eyes
Flee, break free and
Drop from my eyes.
Splash onto my trainers
Splish, splash,
Spatter, splatter.

How Could You?

Davey's mum refused
To let her son come
Back to a school
Where anyone could do that
To her boy.

Davey's mum said
She'd have to be dead,
Before her son
Came back to a school
Where anyone could do that
To her boy.

Davey's mum was more
Than ready, willing and able
To move house if she had to
To move cities if she had to
To move abroad if she had to

Before her son
Came back to a school
Where anyone could do that
To her boy.

Davey's Gone

I went to visit Davey in hospital.
I took him some grapes
And a couple of Spiderman comics
And my favourite science fiction book
That I didn't lend to anyone
Except good friends,
Best friends.

I went with my mum to the hospital.
Mum chatted to Davey's mum
Whilst Davey sat up in bed
Eating the grapes
And eyeing the comics
And flicking through the pages
Of my science fiction book
That I didn't lend to anyone
Except good friends,
Best friends.

Davey's mum had calmed down by now
Besides, Davey wanted to stay at school,
He didn't want to move to another one.
'Why not?' asked his mum.
'Because,' was all Davey would say.
'Because isn't a reason,' said his mum.
Davey shrugged. He'd said everything
He wanted to say. No more. No less.
He looked at me. And there were no sparkles
Or smiles or sideways thoughts in his eyes.
He looked at me, the way everyone else
Looked at me. No more. No less.

'What d'you think of these curtains, Davey?'
I asked desperately. Where had the old
   Davey
Gone? 'They're OK,' shrugged Davey.
OK? They were more than OK.

The hospital curtains around his bed were
Swirls of living colour, shouting scarlets,
Yelling yellows, booming blues, gargling
    greens.
Up and down and round and round
Dancing, melting, merging around each
    other.
Hipping, hopping, tapping, bopping
Alive.
'They're OK,' Davey said again.
Where had the old Davey gone?

OK

I knocked for Davey today.
'Wanna go to the park?' I said.
'OK,' he nodded.
OK . . . I don't like that word.

We walked to the park in silence.
'How're you feeling?' I said.
'OK,' he shrugged.
There was that word again.

The park wasn't too busy.
'Fancy a game of football?' I asked.
'OK,' he replied.
That word again and again.

I glanced around.
Find something quick.
'Or would you rather muck around
In the adventure playground?'

'Fine. OK,' said Davey.
'No, it's not OK!' I shouted.
'Stop saying that word.
I hate that word.'

'What d'you want me to say?'
asked Davey.
'I don't care. As long as it's
Not OK!' I barked at him.

'And what's wrong with OK?'
asked Davey.
'It's boring. It's nothing.
It's not you,' I tried to explain.

But the words in my head
Didn't make any sense.
Except that Davey wasn't OK.
So why say the word?

'But this is what my mum wants,
And this is what you want,
And this is what the whole world
    wants.
I'm the same as everyone else,'
Said Davey. 'I'm OK.'

Davey turned and walked away.
'Where're you going?' I asked.
'Home,' Davey replied.
'I don't belong here.'
And as I watched him go
I felt like I was letting
Liquid sunshine trickle
Through my fingers.

I wanted to call him back
But I knew he wouldn't come.
I checked the grass for glass
And other nasty things.
And when I found a patch
Of grass and nothing else
I sat down and thought.
Then lay down with my eyes closed.

When I opened my eyes,
Clouds filled them.
Clouds so near
I could almost reach out
And touch them.
Time to go cloud busting.
Two was better than one
But one would have to do.

Cloud busting
Staring upwards
Letting the clouds
Fill, not just my eyes
But my ears and my mouth
And my nose. Touching
The clouds. Breathing them,
Sensing them. Being them.

Davey taught me how to do that.

WHAT SHOULD'VE HAPPENED

So I pointed straight up.
'You look like a rabbit
With long, fluffy ears.
And you're a cow's head
Winking at me.
And you . . .'
'That one doesn't look anything like
A cow's head!' said Davey.

He'd come back.
He lay down beside me.
'That one looks like
A table with two vases on it.'
'Don't talk wet! It's a cow's head.'
'A table.'
'A cow's head.'
'A table.'

'You need glasses,' I told him.
'I invented cloud busting,'
Said Davey. 'So what I say goes.'
'But you're not the only one
With an imagination,' I replied.
'You two OK?' asked a woman
Walking by.
'No, we're better than OK,' I told her.

'We're fantastic.'
'We're terrific.'
'We're tremendous.'
'We're stupendous.'
'The grass is wet
We may be rusting
But we're having fun
Cloud busting.'

The woman gave us a funny look
And walked off.
And Davey and I looked at each other
And burst out laughing.
'And we're best friends,'
I shouted after her.
'Secret best friends,' Davey said,
His smile fading.

'Not any more,' I told him.
I stood up and shouted
With all the breath in my body
And all the power in my throat,
'Dave is my best friend.
So what d'you think of that then?'
'Good for you!' An old man
Shouted back at us.

WHAT DID HAPPEN

I lay still, cloud busting.
On my own.
Myself.
Alone.
Me.
I.

AFTER

Davey and I still spoke
Still walked to school
Still played together sometimes
But it was never the same.

He was one of them now.
The same as Alex,
Pete, Barry. He talked
About football and sport.

He played computer games
And read the occasional book.
But any music he didn't like
Was a waste of energy.

And any book he didn't read
Was a waste of time.
And any person he didn't like
Was a waste of space.

He started hanging out with
Alex and the others,
Like a loose-fitting shirt.
Not one of them

But not so apart any more.
Not like me.
And Alex allowed this.
Like a kindly king,

So everyone said.
Like a guilty king
Ashamed and wary,
I thought, my thoughts my own.

Alex was showing the world
He could be generous
He could be noble
He could be better than me.

Davey started hanging out
With Alex and the others.
The ones who used to hang around
With me – a lifetime ago.

And everyone forgot
About Alex and the peanut
But no one forgot
About Davey and me.

AWAY

Davey became me.
And I became him.
I look at the summer sky
And see the bottom of
Heaven's ocean.

I look at a tree
And stand and stare
As the branches
Like arms
Beckon me near.

I look up at the stars
And see holes in
The floor of heaven.
A light so bright
It burns my heart.

I look at people's faces
And see myself in their
Selections of expressions.
Reflections.
Contact.

And my friends drifted away
Walked away
Ran away – including Dave –
Because I wasn't Sam
Any more.

Davey left school
Six months after his
Allergic reaction.
His mum got a better job
In another town.

Davey didn't tell anyone,
He just left.
One week he was there
The next week
He was gone.

And he never said goodbye.
Not to me.
Not to anyone.
He just left.
But he'd already gone.

HOMEWORK

So there you have it, Mr Mackie.
This is my homework
About my best friend, Davey
Who used to be called Fizzy Feet.
And how he went away.

But he left something behind
A thought, a feeling, an idea,
A different way to look at the world.
He left something behind, Mr Mackie.
He left me.

And I'm not Davey as he was.
And I'm not Sam as I was.
I'm Sam here and now.
And I hold out my hands every day
And spin round and round and say,

Isn't life cherry ice cream with chunky
　　chocolate chips?
Isn't life a theme park, a rolling, rip-roaring
　　rollercoaster ride?
Isn't life all the shades of the rainbow
　　seeping through every pore?
Isn't life roast lamb and Mum's rice with
　　slices of cucumber on the side?
Isn't life pop music, class music, a box of
　　paints and a world through each door?
Isn't life a burst of light, a scent to delight,
　　a phoenix rising, dazzling in the night?
Isn't life a magnificent mountain peak or
　　silent woods or warm waves lapping a sandy
　　shore?
Isn't life anything, everything you make it and
　　then much, much, so much, oh much,
　　more?

ABOUT THE AUTHOR

MALORIE BLACKMAN is acknowledged as one of today's most imaginative and convincing writers for young readers. Her book *Noughts & Crosses* won the Children's Book Award, the Sheffield Children's Book Award and the Lancashire Children's Book Award and was voted one of the top 100 titles in the BBC's Big Read. Her previous books for Random House Children's Books include *Hacker*, *Thief!*, *A.N.T.I.D.O.T.E.*, *Dangerous Reality*, *Dead Gorgeous* and *Pig-Heart Boy*, which was shortlisted for the Carnegie Medal and adapted into a BAFTA-award-winning TV serial. Both *Hacker* and *Thief!* won the Young Telegraph/Gimme 5 Award – Malorie is the only author to have won this twice – and *Hacker* also won the WH Smith Mind-Boggling Books Award in 1994.

She has also written a number of titles for younger readers.

Voted Voice/Excelle Children's Writer of the Year in 1997, Malorie lives with her husband and daughter in South London, along with a large collection of books – over 12,000 at the last count!

A NOTE FROM THE AUTHOR

I started writing poems for my own amusement long before I began to write stories. Nursery rhymes, playground songs and pop songs were as much a part of my life as breathing. I was reading at an early age, but this was a deliberate, though fun activity. Reading was something I had to be taught, something I had to sit down and do. Poetry was different. Poetry for me was in the way the branches of a tree danced in the wind, in the way snow fell to the ground bringing silence with it, in running water, in smiles, in music, in skipping songs, in insults, in chants – poetry was everywhere.

In *Cloud Busting*, I used many different forms of poetry as inspiration – haikus, blank verse, limericks, a shape poem. I hasten to add that these were used for inspiration – I didn't stick rigidly to their forms (which are discussed below in more detail). I wanted most of the poems in *Cloud Busting* to be free-form and fluid. I wanted it to sound as if you're really inside the head of Sam, who is telling the story in his own way, without worrying about whether or not his poems conform to a particular style or rhyme.

HAIKUS

Haikus traditionally have seventeen syllables. They are set out in three lines, the first with five syllables, the second with seven, the third with five. Chapter 3 is told entirely in haikus. Strictly speaking, haikus should include a seasonal theme and capture a moment in nature or time. Traditionally, haikus are used for learning and teaching, especially in Zen Buddhism. My verses in Chapter 3 are not strict haikus because some of my sentences follow on and they shouldn't!

LIMERICKS

A limerick is a poem of five lines. The rhyming scheme is a-a-b-b-a. Lines one, two and five have seven to ten syllables and lines three and four have five to seven syllables. In Chapter 5, once again, I don't stick rigidly to the limerick syllable structure.

BLANK VERSE

Chapter 7 is based on blank verse, i.e. unrhymed five-stress lines (iambic pentameters). What that means is each line has ten syllables, which can be split into five pairs with the rhythm, dee-dum, dee-dum, dee-dum, dee-dum, dee-dum. It's said to be the nearest verse form to the rhythms of speech.

SHAPE POEMS

I love shape poems. They're about fitting words not just to a shape but to a relevant meaning as well. There's not much point in writing a poem about a dog and shaping it like a pineapple – unless, of course, that's the point of the poem!

TITLES

In *Cloud Busting*, I use each chapter title as part of the meaning of the chapter. I wanted to make every word count.

I hope you like *Cloud Busting*. Perhaps it will inspire you to write your own poems.